Calumny Refuted By Facts From Liberia

by

Wilson Armistead

Calumny Refuted By Facts From Liberia
by Wilson Armistead

ISBN: 978-93-60463-99-1

Published by

DOUBLE 9 BOOKS

2/13-B, Ansari Road
Daryaganj, New Delhi – 110002
info@double9books.com
www.double9books.com
Tel. 011-40042856

ABOUT THE AUTHOR

Wilson Armistead was a Quaker, businessman, abolitionist, and writer from Leeds. He was born on August 30, 1819, and died on February 18, 1868. He was in charge of the Leeds Anti-Slavery Association and wrote and edited books that were against slavery. His most famous work, A Tribute for the Negro, came out in 1848. In it, he calls slavery "the most extensive and extraordinary system of crime the world has ever witnessed." In 1851, he took in Ellen and William Craft and listed them on the census as "fugitive slaves." This has been called "guerrilla inscription." Abolitionist William Wells Brown, an important African American, said, "Few English gentlemen have done more to hasten the day of the slave's liberation than Wilson Armistead." Wilson Armistead was born on August 30, 1819, in Leeds to Joseph and Hannah Armistead. He grew up in Holbeck, where his family ran a flax and mustard business at Water Hall. The Quaker meeting house was close by on Water Lane. Wilfred Allott said that the Armistead family had been "faithful Friends" for a long time. Armistead married Mary Bragg in 1844, and in 1846, their son Joseph John was born.

CONTENTS

NOTICE TO THE READER

The Reader will please to observe, that the following pages are printed solely with a view of refuting the calumnious charge of incapability and inferiority made against the Negro race, and not for the purpose of vindicating the American Colonization Scheme, concerning which great diversity of opinion exists.

No one can object to the Colonization of Africa, so long as it is *perfectly voluntary* on the part of those who go out as Colonists; in which case, connected with legitimate commerce and plans of civil and Christian improvement, great benefit may accrue; and which, *for the sake of Africa,* is worthy of encouragement. But, to hold up such a scheme, merely as a mode of expatriating the whole of the African race from America, merits the strongest disapprobation.

If "the aristocracy of the skin" were laid aside, and the Coloured population of America were invested with the full rights of citizenship, and every civil prize, every useful employment, and every honourable station were thrown open to their exertions, there can be little doubt, as J. J. Gurney observes, in his Remarks on a Speech of Henry Clay's, "that the mixture of colours, in the same population, would soon be found *perfectly harmless.* Every man, white or black, would rest on his own responsibility; character, like other things, would find its natural level; light and truth would spread without obstruction; and the North American Union would afford, to an admiring world, a splendid and *unsullied* evidence of the truth of that mighty principle on which her constitution is founded; viz., that, 'All men are created EQUAL, and are endowed by the Creator with certain INALIENABLE rights,—Life, Liberty, and the Pursuit of Happiness.'"

W. A.

Leeds, 10th Mo., 1848.

CALUMNY REFUTED

ETC., ETC.

Amidst the numerous attempts to depreciate the character of the Negro, by exhibiting it as inferior and incapable of improvement, it is desirable to adduce evidence of an opposite nature, and to show that circumstances operate no less powerfully on the Sable inhabitants of a tropical climate, than on the natives of more northern latitudes, in which opportunities have been employed to remove the ignorance of uncivilised man, and to invest him with the glorious light of religion and science. How have they raised the brutal to the rational—the degraded to the noble—the idolatrous to the Christian character! What was once the condition of Druidical Britain, when, in the most barbarous manner, parents sacrificed their offspring to senseless deities? And to what can her present position amongst the nations be attributed, but to that expansion of knowledge, human and divine, with which she has been pre-eminently favoured?

The false philosophy which has imputed to the Negro a constitutional inferiority, is amply refuted by facts. There is not only abundant evidence, that the African is susceptible of all the finest feelings of our nature, but that his intellectual capacity, under circumstances more favourable than have generally fallen to his lot, will bear a comparison with that of any other portion of our species.

The capabilities of this calumniated race have been remarkably exhibited within a few years, on a portion of the Western coast of Africa colonised by Free Blacks from the United States, most of them formerly Slaves, including aborigines recaptured from slave-vessels as well as Negroes from the adjoining districts. From this interesting locality, recently constituted into the Free Republic of Liberia, overwhelming evidence might be adduced of the ability, sound judgment, and Christian character of its Sable inhabitants and legislators. Probably no government exists founded more nearly on Christian principles; and the community in general is perhaps as purely moral as any in the world.

Several public schools have been established in the country, and all parents and guardians are required to send their children to them, or be subject to a pecuniary fine; so that there is scarcely a child over six years old that cannot both read and write. The state of religion and morality amongst the people is progressive. The exertion of the authorities has been directed to the exclusion of ardent spirits. A short time ago, one of the colonists assisted in procuring a barrel of rum, which was landed twelve miles distant from the colony; he was fined one hundred dollars, deprived of his license as a trader, and considered no longer eligible to any office in the colony. Such are the stringent efforts to keep down a vice, which, if once suffered to exist, would no doubt prove detrimental. Internal improvements keep pace with the increase of commerce, and the steady revenue which arises therefrom, enables the authorities to effect various public improvements.

These are remarkable facts. Here we behold a community of Blacks, in almost a defenceless state, located on the border of a vast country, the swarming inhabitants of which are enshrouded in ignorance;—a regularly organised government, which, though still in comparative embryo, is the germ of what may become a great and powerful nation, the nucleus of a vast political and religious empire, from which may radiate, far into the interior of this land of moral and intellectual degradation, the elevating and ennobling principles of civilization, and the benign and heavenly influences of Christianity.—Liberia, amidst the gloom of midnight darkness which envelopes the minds of the millions of Africa's benighted children, stands as a beacon-light to direct them to the port of freedom and the haven of everlasting rest.

The present governor of Liberia, J. J. Roberts, under discouraging circumstances, left Virginia some ten or twelve years ago, and, unaided by any culture beyond that attainable on the spot, has placed himself among the most prominent of the citizens of the new Republic. His correspondence with the commanders of British cruisers on the coast of Africa, and his state papers, exhibit a superior force of character and diplomatic ability. The inaugural address, annual messages, and speeches of this Coloured statesman, before a Coloured Legislature, are highly interesting and satisfactory.

I was much gratified in reading, a short time ago, a speech delivered in 1846, at Monrovia, the capital of Liberia, by Hilary Teage, a Coloured senator of the infant Republic. Independent of its embracing a beautiful exposition of the history, trials, exertions, and aspirations of the Coloured colonists, it is a continued flow of eloquence, whilst it breathes throughout a truly Christian spirit. When I read it, I concluded the speaker must be a "classical scholar," probably a "graduate in some eastern college." To my surprise, I afterwards ascertained, he had never even *seen* a college, his father having been a Slave in Virginia, which place Hilary Teage left when very young, and went to Liberia, where he received his education. Here he made rapid advances in learning, soon overcoming the difficulties of several languages, both ancient and modern.

The following are extracts from the Inaugural Address of President Roberts, delivered at the first Meeting of the Legislature of the Republic, January 3rd, 1848, followed by the speech of Hilary Teage; which afford striking evidence of the capacity and attainments of Negroes, whose education and life from early boyhood are thoroughly African:—

"It is with great pleasure I avail myself of the occasion, now presented, to express the profound impressions made on me by the call of my fellow-citizens to the station, and the duties, to which I am now about to pledge myself. So distinguished a mark of confidence, proceeding from the deliberate suffrage of my fellow-citizens, would, under any circumstances, have commanded my gratitude, as well as filled me with an awful sense of the trust to be assumed. But I feel particularly gratified at this evidence of the confidence of my fellow-citizens, inasmuch as it strengthens the impression on me, that my endeavours to discharge faithfully the duties which devolved on me as chief Executive officer of the Commonwealth, during the last six years of our political connection with the American Colonization Society, have been favourably estimated. I, nevertheless, meet the responsibilities of this day with feelings of the deepest solicitude. I feel that the present is a momentous period in the history of Liberia; and I assure you, under the various circumstances which give peculiar solemnity to the crisis, I am sensible that both the honour and the responsibility allotted to me, are inexpressibly enhanced.

"We have just entered upon a new and important career. To give effect to all the measures and powers of the government, we have found it necessary to remodel our Constitution and to erect ourselves into an independent State; which, in its infancy, is exposed to numberless hazards and perils, and which can never attain to maturity, or ripen into firmness, unless it is managed with affectionate assiduity, and guarded by great abilities;—I therefore deeply deplore my want of talents, and feel my mind filled with anxiety and uneasiness, to find myself so unequal to the duties of the important station to which I am called.—When I reflect upon the weight and magnitude now belonging to the station, and the many difficulties which, in the nature of things, must necessarily attend it, I feel more like retreating from the responsible position, than attempting to go forward in the discharge of the duties of my office.

"Indeed, gentlemen of the Legislature, if I had less reliance upon your co-operation and the indulgence and support of a reflecting people, and felt less deeply a consciousness of the duty I owe my country and a conviction of the guidance of an all-wise Providence in the management of our political affairs, I should be compelled to shrink from the task. I enter, however, upon the duties assigned me, relying upon your wisdom and virtue to supply my defects; and under the full conviction that my fellow-citizens at large, who, on the most trying occasions, have always manifested a degree of patriotism, perseverance, and fidelity, that would reflect credit upon the citizens of any country, will support the government established by their voluntary consent, and appointed by their own free choice.

"While I congratulate my fellow-citizens on the dawn of a new and more perfect government, I would also remind them of the increased responsibility they too have assumed. Indeed, if there ever was a period in the annals of Liberia, for popular jealousy to be awakened, and popular virtue to exert itself, it is the present. Other eras, I know, have been marked by dangers and difficulties which 'tried men's souls,' but whatever was their measure, disappointment and overthrow have generally been their fate. The patriotism and virtue which distinguish men, of every age, clime, and colour, who are determined to be free, never forsook that little band of patriots, the pioneers in this noble enterprise, in the hour of important trial. At a time when they were almost without arms, ammunition, discipline, or government—a mere handful of insulated Christian pilgrims, in pursuit of civil and religious liberty, surrounded by savage and warlike tribes bent upon their ruin and total annihilation— with 'a staff and a sling' only, as it were, they determined, in the name of the 'Lord of Hosts,' to stand their ground and defend themselves to the last extremity against their powerful adversary. And need I remind you, fellow-citizens, how signally Almighty God delivered them, and how he has hitherto prospered and crowned all our efforts with success.

"These first adventurers, inspired by the love of liberty and equal rights, supported by industry, and protected by Heaven, became inured to toil, to hardships, and to war. In spite, however, of every obstacle, they obtained a settlement, and happily, under God, succeeded in laying here the foundation of a free government. Their attention, of course, was then turned to the security of those rights for which they had encountered so many perils and inconveniences. For this purpose, a constitution or form of Government, anomalous, it is true, was adopted."

After giving some explanation of the motives which actuated the Colonists in assuming the whole responsibilities of the government of Liberia themselves, President Roberts observes:—

"While we exceedingly lament the want of greater intelligence and more experience to fit us for the proper, or more perfect management of our public affairs,—we flatter ourselves that the adverse circumstances under which we so long laboured in the land of our birth,[1] and the integrity of our motives, will plead excuse for our want of abilities; and that in the candour and charity of an impartial world, our well-meant, however feeble efforts, will find an apology. I am also persuaded, that no magnanimous nation will seek to abridge our rights, or withhold from the Republic those civilities, and 'that comity which marks the friendly intercourse between civilised and independent communities'—in consequence of our weakness and present poverty."

The enlightened Negro legislator, after entering into a consideration and refutation of the charge made against the Colonists, of having acted prematurely in proclaiming their independence, continues:—

"The time has been, I admit, when men—without being chargeable with timidity, or with a disposition to undervalue the capacities of the African race, might have doubted the feasibility of establishing an independent Christian state on this coast, composed of, and conducted wholly by Coloured men,—but, fellow-citizens, that time has passed, and I believe in my soul, that the permanency of the government of the Republic of Liberia is now fixed upon as firm a basis as human wisdom is capable of devising. Nor is there any reason to apprehend that the Divine Disposer of human events, after having separated us from the house of bondage, and led us safely through so many dangers, towards the land of liberty and promise, will leave the work of our political redemption, and consequent happiness, unfinished; and either permit us to perish in a wilderness of difficulties, or suffer us to be carried back in chains to that country of prejudices, from whose oppression He has mercifully delivered us with his out-stretched arm.

"It must afford the most heartfelt pleasure and satisfaction to every friend of Liberia, and real lover of liberty, to observe by what a fortunate train of circumstances and incidents the people of these colonies have arrived at absolute freedom and independence. When we look abroad and see by what slow and painful steps, marked with blood and ills of every kind, other states of the world have advanced to liberty and independence; we cannot but admire and praise that all-gracious Providence, who, by His unerring ways, has, with so few sufferings on our part, compared with other states, led us to this happy stage in our progress towards those great and important objects. That it is the will of Heaven that mankind should be free, is clearly evidenced by the wealth, vigour, virtue, and consequent happiness of all free states. But the idea that Providence will establish such governments as he shall deem most fit for his creatures, and will give them wealth, influence, and happiness, without their efforts, is palpably absurd. God's moral government of the earth is always performed by the intervention of second causes. Therefore, fellow-citizens, while with pious gratitude we survey the frequent interpositions of Heaven in our behalf, we ought to remember, that as the disbelief of an overruling Providence is Atheism, so, an absolute confidence of having our government relieved from every embarrassment, and its citizens made respectable and happy by the immediate hand of God, without our own exertions, is the most culpable presumption. Nor have we any reason to expect, that He will miraculously make Liberia a paradise, and deliver us, in a moment of time, from all the ills and inconveniences consequent upon the peculiar circumstances under which we are placed, merely to convince us that He favours our cause and government.

"Sufficient indications of His will are always given, and those who will not then believe, neither would they believe though one should rise from the dead to inform them. Who can trace the progress of these colonies, and mark the incidents of the wars in which they have been engaged, without seeing evident tokens of Providential favour. Let us, therefore, inflexibly persevere in exerting our most strenuous efforts, in an humble and rational dependence on the great Governor of all the world, and we have the fairest prospects of surmounting all the difficulties which may be thrown in our way. That we may expect, and that we shall have difficulties, sore difficulties yet to contend against, in our progress to maturity, is certain: and, as the political happiness or wretchedness of ourselves and our children, and of generations yet unborn, is in our hands, nay more, the redemption of Africa from the deep degradation, superstition, and idolatry in which she has so long been involved, it becomes us to lay our shoulders to the wheel, and manfully resist every obstacle which may oppose our progress in the great work which lies before us. The Gospel is yet to be preached to vast numbers inhabiting this dark continent, and I have the highest reason to believe, that it was one of the great objects of the Almighty, in establishing these colonies, that they might be the means of introducing civilization and religion among the barbarous nations of this country; and to what work more noble could our powers be applied, than that of bringing up from darkness, debasement, and misery, our fellow-men, and shedding abroad over them the light of science and Christianity. The means of doing so, fellow-citizens, are within our reach, and if we neglect, or do not make use of them, what excuse shall we make to our Creator and final Judge? This is a question of the deepest concern to us all, and which, in my opinion, will materially affect our happiness in the world to come. And surely, if ever it has been incumbent on the people of Liberia to know truth and to follow it, it is now. Rouse, therefore, fellow-citizens, and do your duty like men: and be persuaded, that Divine Providence, as heretofore, will continue to bless all your virtuous efforts.

"But if there be any among us, dead to all sense of honour and love of their country; deaf to all the calls of liberty, virtue, and religion; forgetful of the benevolence and magnanimity of those who have procured this asylum for them, and the future happiness of their children; if neither the examples nor the success of other nations, the dictates of reason and of nature, nor the great duties they owe to their God, themselves, and their posterity, have no effect upon them;— if neither the injuries they received in the land whence they came, the prize they are contending for, the future blessings or curses of their children, the applause or reproach of all mankind, the approbation or displeasure of the great Judge, nor the happiness or misery consequent upon their conduct, in this and a future state, can move them; then, let them be assured, that they deserve to be Slaves, and are entitled to nothing but anguish and tribulation. Let them banish, for ever, from their minds, the hope of obtaining that freedom, reputation, and happiness, which, as men, they are entitled to. Let them forget every duty, human and divine, remember not that they have children, and beware how they call to mind the justice of the Supreme Being: let them return into Slavery, and hug their chains, and be a reproach and a by-word among all nations.

"But I am persuaded, that we have none such among us;— that every citizen will do his duty, and exert himself to the utmost of his abilities to sustain the honour of his country, promote her interests, and the interests of his fellow-citizens, and to hand down unimpaired to future generations, the freedom and independence we this day enjoy.

"As to myself, I assure you, I have never been indifferent to what concerns the interests of Liberia—my adopted country; and I am sensible of no passion which could seduce me, knowingly, from the path of duty or of justice: the weakness of human nature, and the limits of my own understanding may, no doubt will, produce errors of judgment.—I repeat, therefore, that I shall need the indulgence I have hitherto received at your hands. I shall need, too, the favour of that Being in whose hands we are, who has led us, as Israel of old, from our native land, and planted us in a country abounding in all the necessaries and comforts of life; who has covered our infancy with his providence, and to whose goodness I ask you to join with me in supplications, that He will so enlighten the minds of your servants, guide their councils, and prosper their measures, that whatsoever they do shall result in your good, and shall secure to you the peace, friendship, and approbation of all nations."

Anniversary Speech of Hilary Teage, a Coloured gentleman, (the son of a Virginian Slave), delivered at Monrovia, in Liberia, December 1st, 1846:—

"Fellow-Citizens:—As far back towards the infancy of our race, as history and tradition are able to conduct us, we have found the custom every where prevailing among mankind, to mark, by some striking exhibition, those events which were important and interesting, either in their immediate bearing or in their remote consequences upon the destiny of those among whom they occurred. These events are epochs in the history of man—they mark the rise and fall of kingdoms and of dynasties—they record the movements of the human mind, and the influence of those movements upon the destinies of the race; and whilst they frequently disclose to us the sad and sickening spectacle of innocence bending under the weight of injustice, and of weakness robbed and despoiled by the hand of an unscrupulous oppression; they occasionally display, as a theme for admiring contemplation, the sublime spectacle of the human mind, roused by a concurrence of circumstances, to vigorous advances in the career of improvement. To trace the operations of these circumstances from their first appearance, as effects from the workings of the human passions, until, as a cause, they revert with combined and concentrated energy upon those minds from which they at first evolved, would be at once a most interesting and difficult task; and, let it be borne in mind, requires far higher ability and more varied talent than he possesses who this day has the honour to address you.

"The utility of thus marking the progress of time—of recording the occurrence of events—and of holding up remarkable personages to the contemplation of mankind, is too obvious to need remark. It arises from the instincts of mankind—the irrepressible spirit of emulation—and the ardent longings after immortality; and this restless passion to perpetuate their existence, which they find it impossible to suppress, impels them to secure the admiration of succeeding generations in the performance of deeds, by which, although dead, they may yet speak. In commemorating events thus powerful in forming the manners and sentiments of mankind, and in rousing them to strenuous exertion and to high and sustained emulation, it is obvious that such, and such only, should be selected as virtue and humanity would approve; and that, if any of an opposite character be held up, they should be displayed only as beacons, or as a towering Pharos throwing a strong but lurid light to mark the melancholy grave of mad ambition, and to warn the inexperienced voyager of the existing danger.

"Thanks to the improved and humanised spirit—or, should I not rather say, the chastened and pacific civilization of the age in which we live,—that laurels gathered upon the field of mortal strife, and bedewed with the tears of the Widow and the Orphan, are regarded now, not with admiration but with horror—that the armed warrior, reeking with the gore of murdered thousands, who, in the age that is just passing away, would have been hailed with noisy acclamation by the senseless crowd, is now regarded only as the savage commissioner of an unsparing oppression, or at best as the ghostly executioner of an unpitying justice.—He who would embalm his name in the grateful remembrance of coming generations—he who would secure for himself a niche in the temple of undying fame—he who would hew out for himself a monument of which his country may boast—he who would entail upon heirs a name which they may be proud to wear, must seek some other field than that of battle as the theatre of his exploits.

"Still, we honour the heroes of the age that has passed. No slander can tarnish their hard-earned fame—no morbid sentimentalism sully their peerless glory—no mean detraction abate the disinterestedness of their conduct. They bowed to the spirit of their age: and, acting up to the light afforded them, they yielded to the dictates of an honest conscience. While assembled here to-day, on this festal occasion, to commemorate the event for which the founders of our infant Republic toiled, and fought, and bled, we seem to behold the forms of the departed ones mingling in our assembly: we seem to behold them taking their seats by the side of their venerable compeers yet spared among us: watching with intense anxiety the emotions which agitate our bosoms, and marking the character of the resolves which the occasion is ripening. Rest in peace, ye venerable shades! And ye, their living representatives—calm be the evening of your days. We honour you. And though no sculptured marble transmit your fame, a nobler monument shall be yours—the happy hearts of unborn millions shall be the shrine in which your names will be treasured. In your high example—in your noble disinterestedness—in your entire subordination of every thought, and act, and scheme, and interest, to the heaven-born purpose of human regeneration and human elevation, we hear the language of encouragement.

"Fellow-citizens,—on this occasion, so big with subjects of profitable meditation—when it is so natural that the mind should oscillate between the events of the past and the prospects of the future, we can conceive of nothing more proper than the enquiry, how we can best execute the solemn trust committed to our hand—how we may challenge and secure the admiration and the gratitude of a virtuous and a happy posterity, by transmitting to them the patrimony received from our fathers, not only in all its original entireness, but in vastly augmented beauty, order, and strength. In a word, how we may best conduct ourselves so as to encite them to high and sustained exertion in the cause of virtue and humanity.

"In order to impress your minds with the propriety of this enquiry, there is, I trust, no need that I shall remind you of the peculiarity of our condition. It will suffice that I remark, that, should you succeed in rearing upon the foundation already laid,—or, to drop the figure—should you succeed in establishing a community of virtuous, orderly, intelligent, and industrious citizens, this very peculiarity must enter largely into every consideration on the amount of praise to which you shall be held entitled.

"Let us, then, for a moment look back, that from the events of the past we may derive hope for the future.

"We have not yet numbered twenty-six years since he who is the oldest colonist amongst us was the inhabitant—not the citizen—of a country—and that too the country of his birth—where the prevailing sentiment is, that he and his race are incapacitated, by an inherent defect in their mental constitution, to enjoy that greatest of all blessings, and to exercise that greatest of all rights, bestowed by a beneficent

God upon his rational creatures—namely, the government of themselves. Acting upon this opinion—an opinion as false as it is foul—acting upon this opinion, as upon a self-evident proposition, those who held it proceeded with a fiendish consistency to deny the rights of citizens to those whom they had declared incapable of performing the duties of citizens. It is not necessary, and therefore I will not disgust you with the hideous picture of that state of things which followed upon the prevalence of this blasphemous opinion. The bare mention that such an opinion prevailed, would be sufficient to call up in the mind, even of those who had never witnessed its operation, images of the most sickening and revolting character. Under the iron reign of this crushing sentiment, most of us who are assembled here to-day, drew our first breath and sighed away the years of our youth. No hope cheered us: no noble object looming in the dim and distant future kindled our ambition. Oppression—cold, cheerless oppression, like the dreary region of an eternal winter, chilled every noble passion and fettered and paralysed every arm. And if among the oppressed millions there were found here and there one in whose bosom the last glimmer of a generous passion was not yet extinguished—one, who, from the midst of the inglorious slumberers in the deep degradation around him, would lift his voice and demand those rights which the God of nature hath bestowed in equal gift upon all His rational creatures, he was met at once by those who had at first denied and then enforced, with the stern reply, that for him and for all his race—Liberty and Expatriation are inseparable.

"Dreadful as the alternative was—fearful as was the experiment now proposed to be tried, there were hearts equal to the task—hearts which quailed not at the dangers which loomed and frowned in the distance, but calm, cool, and fixed in their purpose, prepared to meet them with the watchword—Give me Liberty or give me Death.

"On the 6th day of February, in the year of Our Lord One Thousand Eight Hundred and Twenty, the ship Elizabeth cast loose from her moorings at New York, and on the 8th day of March, of the same year, the pilgrims first beheld the land of their fathers, the cloud-capped mountains of Sierra Leone, and cast anchor in that harbour. A few days afterwards they again weighed anchor, stood to the south, and debarked upon the low and deadly island of Sherbro. On the character of those who formed her noble company, I deem it unnecessary to remark. They are sufficiently commended to our esteem, as being the first to encounter the difficulties and to face the dangers of an enterprise, which, we trust, is to wipe away from us the reproach of ages—to silence the calumny of those who abuse us, and to restore to Africa her long-lost glory. I need not detain you with a narrative of their privations and sufferings: nor will I stop to tell you—though it would be a pleasing task to do so—with what happy hearts they greeted a reinforcement of pilgrims who joined them in 1821, by the Nautilus. Passing by intermediate events, which, did the time allow, it would be interesting to notice, we hasten to that grand event—that era of our separate existence, the 25th day of April, in the year of Grace 1822, when the American flag first threw out its graceful folds to the breeze on the heights of Mesurado, and the pilgrims, relying upon the protection of Heaven and the moral grandeur of their cause, took solemn possession of the land in the name of virtue, humanity, and religion.

"It would discover an unpardonable apathy, were we to pass on without pausing a moment to reflect upon the emotions which heaved the bosoms of the pilgrims, when they stood for the first time where we now stand. What a prospect spread out before them!! They stood in the midst of an ancient wilderness, rank and compacted by the growth of a thousand years, unthinned and unreclaimed by a single stroke of the woodman's axe. Few and far between might be found inconsiderable openings, where the ignorant native erected his rude habitation, or, savage as his patrimonial wilderness, celebrated his bloody rites, and presented his votive gifts, to Demons. Already the late proprietors of the soil had manifested unequivocal symptoms of hostility, and an intention to expel the strangers, as soon as an opportunity to do so should be presented. The rainy season, that terrible ordeal of foreign constitutions, was about setting in; the lurid lightning shot its fiery bolt into the forest around them; the thunder muttered its angry tones over their head; and the frail tenements, the best which their circumstances would afford, to shield them from a scorching sun by day and drenching rains at night, had not yet been completed. To suppose that at this time, when all things above and around them seemed to combine their influences against them, to suppose they did not perceive the full danger and magnitude of the enterprise they had embarked in, would be to suppose, not that they were heroes, but that they had lost the sensibility of men. True courage is equally remote from blind recklessness and unmanning timidity; and true heroism does not consist in insensibility to danger. He is a hero who calmly meets, and fearlessly grapples the dangers which duty and honour forbid him to decline. The pilgrims rose to a full perception of all the circumstances of their condition. But when they looked back to that country from which they had come out, and remembered the degradations in that house of bondage out of which they had been so fortunate as to escape, they bethought themselves; and, recollecting the high satisfaction with which they knew success would gladden their hearts, the rich inheritance they would entail upon their children, and the powerful aid it would lend to the cause of universal humanity, they yielded to the noble inspiration and girded them to the battle, either for doing or for suffering.

"Let it not be supposed, because I have laid universal humanity under a tribute of gratitude to the founders of Liberia, that I have attached to their humble achievements too important an influence, in that grand system of agencies which is now at work, renovating human society, and purifying and enlarging the sources of its enjoyment. In the system of that Almighty Being, without whose notice not a sparrow falls to the ground:

> 'Who sees with equal eye, as God of all,
>
> A hero perish, or a sparrow fall:
>
> Atoms or systems into ruin hurled,
>
> And now a bubble burst, and now a world:'

—In the system of the Almighty One, no action of a mortal being is unimportant. Every action of every rational creature hath its assigned place in his system of operations, and is made to bear, however undesigned by the agent, with force upon the end which His wisdom and goodness have in view to accomplish.

"On the morning of the 1st day of December, in the year of Our Lord One Thousand Eight Hundred and Twenty-two; on that morning, just when the gloom of night was retiring before the advancing light of day, the portentous cloud which had been some time rising upon the horizon of Liberia, increasing and gathering blackness as it advanced, filling all hearts with fearful apprehension, burst upon the colony with the force of a tornado. The events of that day have marked it as the most conspicuous in our annals, and it is the anniversary of that day we are here assembled to celebrate.

"And what, fellow-citizens, are the particular circumstances of that most eventful day which more than others awaken our exultation? On which one amongst them all is our attention most intensely fixed? Is it on that our fathers fought, and fought bravely, and strewed the ensanguined plain with the dead bodies of their savage assailants? Is it on the bloody lesson of their superiority which they taught them in the hoarse thunder of the murderous cannon? Is it on that greater skill they displayed in the inglorious art of slaughter and death? I trust not. These trophies of their valour serve not to awaken exultation, but to call up a sigh of regret. It was as the possessors of far higher and nobler virtues they desired to be remembered; as such we tenderly cherish the remembrance of them; and to exult over the fallen foe would be to grieve the pure spirit of those by whose arm the savage fell. Necessity, stern necessity, unsheathed their sword and forced upon them an alternative from which all the feelings of their heart turned with instinctive recoil.

"But there is a circumstance connected with the events of that day, with which our hearts cannot be too deeply impressed, as it will serve, on each appropriate occasion, as a check upon presumption and an antidote against despair. Think upon the number of the assailants, and compare it with the number of the assailed, and then say whether any scepticism short of downright, unblushing Atheism, can doubt the interposition, in the events of that day, of an overruling Providence. Most emphatically does the issue of that contest declare, 'The battle is not to the strong.' The Lord was a shield around them, so that when their foes rose up against them, they stumbled and fell. To the interposition of an ever-gracious Providence, manifested in no ordinary way, we owe the privileges and pleasure of this day.

"At this epoch we date the establishment of the colony.

"Having sustained and repulsed every external attack, and maintained its ground against the combined and concentrated forces of the country, it had now to commence its onward career. If there were any, who, because the colonists had repulsed the natives, supposed they had passed the greatest danger, and overcome the most formidable obstacles, they gave, in this very supposition, evidence of a deplorable ignorance of human nature and of human history. It is from within, that the elements of national overthrow have most commonly evolved: and the weakness under which nations expire, generally results from disease of the national heart. Luxury and ambition, oppression on the one side and insubordination on the other; these are the fatal elements which, with more than volcanic force, rend to atoms the fabric of human institutions. A common danger, a danger equally menacing all, is almost sure to sink every minor and merely personal consideration, and to be met by a combination of energy, concentration of effort, and unity of action: and in proportion as the pressure of the danger is great, will there be want of scope for those passions which, in a certain class, possess such fearful and disorganising potency.

"From the period of their landing, up to the moment of which we have just spoken, all minds had been possessed by an undefined apprehension of impending danger, and the first and the constant lesson which their critical position inculcated upon them was, Union and Subordination. The pressure was now taken off, the angry cloud had now passed away, the heavens shone bright and clear, the face of nature was calm and placid, and on every breeze was wafted the fragrance from the surrounding groves. All breathed freely. Each one had time to look around him, to contemplate with calmness and composure the circumstances of his condition, and to select that particular mode of operation, and line of conduct, which was most congenial with his disposition. All were free; All were equal. Here was unbounded scope for the operation of the passions. Will they, who have been declared incapable of enjoying liberty without running into the wildest excesses of anarchy—will they, now the gift is enjoyed in its largest extent, restrain themselves within the bounds of a rational and virtuous freedom? Will they connect those two ideas which are at one and the same time the base and the summit of all just political theories, and which can never be separated? Will their liberty be tempered by just and wholesome law? Is it to be expected that a people just set free from the chains of the most abject oppression and slavery, can be otherwise than turbulent, insubordinate, and impatient of the least restraint? Is it among the things to be hoped, that they into whose minds the idea of political action had not been allowed to enter, will not, now political power is entrusted to their hands, rush into the wildest extremes of crude legislation?

"Fellow-Citizens! the voice of twenty-four years this day gives the answer; and we are assembled to hear it, and let those who abuse us hear it; let them hear it and be for ever silent, when they hear that Liberty regulated by Law, and Religion free from Superstition, form the foundation on which rests the cement which unites, and the ornament which beautifies, our political and social edifice.

"Let us now turn from those who preceded us, and ask, What are the peculiar obligations which rest upon us: what the particular duties to which we are called? Let us not suppose, that because we are not called upon to drive the invading native from our door—that because we can lie down at night without fear—because the savage war-whoop does not now ring upon the midnight air,—therefore we have nothing to do. No mistake can be more fatal. Ours is a moral fight. It is a keener warfare, a sharper conflict.

"For, after indulging to the utmost allowed extent in hyperbolical expression and figurative declamation, still we are forced to confess, the work is but just commenced. The nervous arm of our predecessor marked out the site, and laid the foundation, and reared the walls, of the edifice. The scaffold is still around it. It is ours to mount it—to commence where they ended, and to conduct it on towards a glorious completion. How shall we execute our trust— how shall we conduct ourselves so as to stand acquitted before the bar of coming generations, and obtain from them a favourable and an honorable verdict? By what means shall we secure and perpetuate our own prosperity, and transmit it an inheritance to our children? These are questions which seem peculiarly appropriate to this interesting occasion. And let me congratulate you, fellow-citizens, that you have the experience of others to guide you. The art of government is now elevated to the dignity of a science. The most gifted minds—minds which do honour to human nature, have long been turned to the subject: and maxims and propositions which, consecrated by time, had grown into the strength of axioms—maxims which had obtained universal assent and universal application—maxims which would have overwhelmed him who should have doubted them, with more than sacrilegious turpitude and sent him to atone for his presumption upon the scaffold, or in the gloomy depths of a dungeon—maxims the legitimate offspring of ignorance and oppression, have been successfully explored and the human mind disenthralled. That more than magical phrase, in the hand of the despot, 'the divine right of kings,' has lost its power to charm; and frequent examinations into the foundations of society have at length taught men the interesting truth, that the duties and rights of magistrate and subject are correlate—that government is made for the people, and not the people for the government: thus establishing the eternal truth first enunciated in the Declaration of American Independence, 'That all men are free and equal.' The bare utterance of those ever-memorable words, by the immortal Jefferson, whilst it struck the fetters from the human mind, and sent it bounding on in a career of improvement, wrested the sceptre from the tyrant's hand and dissolved his throne beneath him. 'Magna est veritas et prævalebit.'[2]—Truth threw a strong and steady light where there was naught but darkness before: man beheld his dignity and his rights, and prepared to demand the one and sustain the other. But I return. By what means shall we advance our prosperity?

"The first requisite, to permanent advancement, if I may so speak, is order. Order is heaven's first law. It is this which imparts stability to human institutions, because, while like the laws of nature it restrains each one in his proper sphere, it leaves all to operate freely and without disturbance. Here will be no jostling. When I say order, I mean not to restrict the term to the ordinary occupations of life; I extend the word to mean, a strict and conscientious submission to established law. It is said to be the boast of that form of government under which we live, that no man, however high in office, can violate with impunity the sacred trust committed to his hand, and long insult the people by trampling upon their rights: that the distinguishing excellence of a republican form of government is, that, under it, oppression can have no place. This opinion I am not disposed to combat; but as it is a fact, that a safe and constitutional remedy for all grievances of this kind is in the hands of the people, this circumstance alone should dispose every one to submit, for a time, to some inconvenience rather than apply a rash and violent corrective. I admit, there are cases in which the minions of office become so intoxicated with a little brief power—that, forgetting all men are free and possess certain constitutional privileges, and forgetting also, that they were elevated to office not to be oppressors but conservators, their haughty, vexatious, and oppressive conduct, becomes intolerable. In such cases as these, let the strong indignation of an outraged public, calmly but firmly expressed, awaken the dreamer from his vision of greatness, and send him back to re-enact his dream in his original obscurity.

"Another argument for order and subordination lies in the fact, that the laws are in the hands of the people. Legislators are not elevated to office for their private emolument and honour, but for the nobler purpose of advancing and securing the happiness of their constituents: and they are bound—by the most solemn considerations—they are bound, to enact such laws, and such laws only, as are suited to the genius and circumstances of the people. If they betray the high trust committed to them, and enact laws either oppressive or partial, the corrective is equally in the hands of the people. They have only to apply the constitutional remedy. Here, then, is no apology for disorder. Order, then, must be our rule; for without subordination, and prompt and constant and conscientious obedience to wholesome law, there can be no security for person nor property. The bands of society would be untwisted, and the whole fabric exposed to ruin on the first popular outbreak. Be it, then, fellow-citizens, our first concern to sustain our officers in the proper discharge of their constitutional duties; to secure obedience to the laws, and to preserve them from violation with the same jealousy with which we watch the first encroachment of power.

"I observe, in the second place, that union among ourselves is absolutely necessary to prosperity. The idea of prosperity and stability where disunion reigns, where the elements of discord are actively at work; the idea of prosperity and stability, in such circumstances, can only serve to mislead. Can that army, in which faction triumphs among the soldiers and disunion and jealousy distract the counsels of the officers, hope to succeed in a campaign? Where each is afraid of the other, where no one has confidence in any, where every one regards every other one with feelings not only of jealousy but of positive hostility, how can there be any hope to bring an unbroken front to bear with undivided force upon any single point? I would observe also, that the complexion of the soldiers' mind will be sure to be tinged by that of their officers. In every community there will be found some few to whom the mass will look up with unenquiring deference. Mankind, generally, are averse to the labour of thinking. This circumstance separates those who should be very friends, and men file off under different leaders as fancy or caprice may dictate. Each party ranges itself under the banner of a leader whom it invests with all perfection of political sagacity and political integrity. To his semi-brutal followers his word is law; his decisions an oracle. Finding in him every attribute of perfection, they abandon the reins to his hand; yield up the glorious privileges of thinking and examining, and prepare to follow with a blind and implicit obedience. This unworthy abandonment of the public interests, this surrender of a privilege to which every man is born, and which every man should exercise, is the capital of intriguing politicians and unprincipled political demagogues. And, let me ask you, fellow-citizens, what scheme, however mad and absurd, which has been set on foot by these unprincipled leaders, has not had among the masses its advocates and adherents? Bad, however, as human nature is, alluring and fascinating as are the glitter and privilege of place and power, this confidence has not been always abused. We could easily point out instances, in which the influence which this disposition we have been adverting to has given to men, has been exerted wholly and exclusively for the public good. But we must take human nature as we find it; and as we find this disposition every where prevalent, the duty becomes imperative on all who have influence, to exert it for the public good. The root of the jealousies and divisions among public men will, generally speaking, be found planted in the soil of selfishness and ambition: not in any real and sincere disagreement as to the proper measures for the public good. This, I admit, is always the avowed, the ostensible, but, I am bold to say, not the real cause.

"It is envy of place and emolument—it is ambition of power, that array public men in a hostile attitude, and range their infatuated followers under their opposing banners. In the infancy of our political existence, let those amongst us who have credit with the people and influence over them, beware of so great infatuation. Let us recollect, that all cannot govern: that from the division and order into which society naturally resolves itself, all even of those who are worthy, cannot stand in the foremost ranks. Let us remember, that we equally serve our country, whether we sit in the gubernatorial or presidential chair; whether we deliberate in the Hall of the Legislature or preside in the Sanctuary of Justice; that we equally serve our country, whether from the shades of cloistered retirement we send forth wholesome maxims for public instruction, or in the intercourse of our daily life we set an attracting example of obedience to the laws; that we equally serve our country, whether from the sacred desk we inculcate lessons of celestial wisdom, exhibit the sanctions of a heaven-descended religion and the thunders of an incensed Jehovah, or in the nursery of learning unfold the mysteries and display the glories of science, recall and re-enact the deeds and the achievements of the past, and call back upon the stage the heroes, the patriots, and the sages of antiquity, to kindle the ardour, nerve the virtue, awaken the patriotism, elevate and purify the sentiment, and expand the mind, of the generous and aspiring youth. Humble as many of those offices of which I have spoken are esteemed to be,— obscure and concealed from vulgar gaze and destitute of the trappings of office and the glitter of fame as most of them actually are, it is, nevertheless, fellow-citizens, not within the reach of our judgment to determine which one of them exerts the greatest influence on the destinies of our race. True dignity, and, I may add, true usefulness, depend not so much upon the circumstance of office as upon the faithful discharge of appropriate duties.

> 'Honour and fame from no condition rise;
>
> Act well your part—there all true honour lies.'

> 'He who does the best his circumstances allow,
>
> Does well, acts nobly: Angels could do no more.'

"It is the false notion of honour which has unhappily possessed the minds of men, placing all dignity in the pageantry of state and the tinsel of office, which produces those collisions, jostlings, and acrimony of contending factions which sometimes shake the fabric of society to its very foundations: it is by the maddening influence of this false notion that men, whose claim to respectful notoriety is inversely as their desire to be conspicuous, are sometimes urged to abandon their obscure but appropriate position in the line, and to rush into the foremost ranks. When men shall have learned wherein true honour lies—when men shall have formed correct ideas of true and sober dignity, then we shall see all the ranks of society united as by a golden chain—then Ephraim shall not envy Judah, nor Judah vex Ephraim;—then the occupant of the palace and of the cottage—then the man in lawn and the man in rags will, like the parts of a well-adjusted machine, act in perfect unison. Considering, then, the influence which in every community a few men are found to possess—considering, also, that each one of these influential men is sure to be followed by a party, we can hardly appreciate the obligation which rests upon them, to abandon all jealousies and suspicions—to merge every private and personal consideration in thoughts for the public good—and to bring a mind untrammelled, and free from every party predilection, to a solemn deliberation on the great objects of public utility.

"The education of our youth is the next subject to which I would direct your attention. 'Knowledge is power'—is an old proverb—but not the less true because it is old. This is the spring that regulates the movements of society—this is at once the lever and the safety-valve of human institutions.

Without it society will either not move at all, or, like an unbalanced, unhelmed ship, move in a direction and at a rate that must eventually destroy it. Education corrects vice—cures disorders—abates jealousies—adorns virtue—commands the winds—triumphs over the waves—scales the heavens. In a word, education lays all nature under tribute, and forces her to administer to the comfort and happiness of man. Nor is this all that education does. It ennobles and elevates the mind, and urges the soul upward and animates it to deeds of high and lasting renown. Education opens sources of pure, refined, and exquisite enjoyment—it unlocks the temple of nature, and admits the awe-stricken soul, to behold and admire the wondrous work of God. An ignorant, vicious, idle community, has the elements of destruction already in its bosom. On the very first application of a torch they will explode and lay the whole fabric in ruins. A virtuous, orderly, educated people, have all the elements of national greatness and national perpetuity.—Would we be happy at home and respected abroad, we must educate our youth.

"In professing to notice those things which are necessary to our prosperity—to the advancement of our prosperity, and the perpetuity of our prosperity, it is natural that you should expect that agricultural industry will be brought prominently into view. I think it may be safely affirmed, that the virtue and independence of a people will be inversely as their attention is wholly given to commerce—that their virtue and independence is evermore to be measured by their pursuits of the wholesome and pleasing and primitive employment of agriculture and husbandry. Go into the countries of Europe—examine their large manufacturing and commercial towns and cities. Then visit the rural, agricultural districts—compare the quiet, tranquillity, order, virtue, plenty of the latter, with the bustle, confusion, vice, and general dependence and poverty of the other, and you cannot fail to be struck, and deeply affected, by the frightful contrast. And wherefore? Is not commerce called the great civiliser of the world? Is it not the means by which nations become acquainted and hold communion with each other? Is it not by this means that the great and master-minds of one nation commune with kindred minds of other nations?

Is it not the channel through which improvements in art, in science, in literature, in all that adorns, dignifies, and ennobles human nature, flow as on the wings of the wind from country to country? Grant it. It is not my purpose to pronounce a wholesale anathema upon commerce. I appreciate its high importance in improving our race. It is excess I would discourage—it is the wretched deteriorating influence it will exert upon a people, when, by absorbing their whole attention, it keeps them looking constantly abroad to the neglect of the improvement of their own country. It is to this I would call your attention. Again;—Let it not be forgotten, that if commerce imports improvements, it imports vices also. It offers the same facility for the transmission of both. The same vessel that brings us the Book of God brings us also the Age of Reason—and in one and the same ship, we not unfrequently find the devoted self-sacrificing missionary, and that accursed thing which a celebrated orator with characteristic energy has styled 'liquid fire and distilled damnation!!'

"In the natural, or, more properly, vegetable world, we have sometimes seen exotics outstripping in rapidity of growth the natural spontaneous productions of the soil. In this we have not a very unhappy illustration of the rank growth of imported vices. These baneful exotics, grafted on the tree of indigenous corruption, seem to receive and impart unwonted vigour from the contact: and the result is, a fruit of the most disorganising potency. An examination into the moral state of towns and districts, wholly given to commerce and manufactures, will fully sustain this remark. How, let me ask you, can there be order, where the very nature of the pursuits which engross all minds demand ceaseless hurry, bustle, and confusion?—where to stop to breathe is to be at once outdone, and where he who can move the most swiftly amid the greatest confusion is thought to be the smartest man! In respect of virtue,—is it to be thought of, except for the purpose of holding it up to ridicule, in a place where the vicious of all countries meet; and where females of every class and character, far from the watchful eye of parental solicitude, are huddled together in one promiscuous throng, and dependent for their daily bread upon the freaks and fancies of unprincipled employers! Lowell, in America, is,

I believe, the only large manufacturing town where virtue is held in the least esteem. What shall I say of honesty and integrity? where the lowest, basest arts, are practised for gain; where all is intrigue and circumvention—where the maxim prevails, 'all is fair in trade'—where each regards the other as lawful game—where one can gain only by the loss of the other—where, in a word, rascality is fair-play, and villainy systematic;—where, fellow-citizens, let me ask you, where, in such a community, is there room for honesty? Can the heart fail, in such circumstances, to become deadened to every feeling of humanity—steeled against every kindly, generous, and ennobling impulse? I will not venture to affirm, that the result we have just now noticed is universal. I admit, with pleasure, there are honourable exceptions— but I do affirm, that what I have said forms the general rule.

"But let us turn from these scenes of noise and smoke and deep depravity, and visit the quiet abode of the farmer and the husbandman. What tranquillity reigns here, and order, and peace, and virtue!! Behold the farmer, as he goes forth in the morning to his daily task;—how firm and elastic his step; how cheerful his sun-burnt countenance; how active his athletic arm!! Behold how cheerfully he labours; how the fat valleys around him laugh with corn; how the spacious plains teem with grain, and the ancient forests fall beneath his resounding axe!! Follow him, when the labour of the day is over, follow him to his humble home. See him surrounded by an affectionate, industrious, frugal wife, unsophisticated by the vices and dissipations of the fashionable world, and by a prattling progeny blooming in health, and big with promise of future usefulness. No cankering cares gnaw his peaceful bosom; no uncertain speculation disturbs his quiet slumbers; no revolutions in foreign lands, damming up the channels of trade, cloud the calm serenity of his brow. Oh! if there be a spot on earth, where true happiness is to be found, here is that spot.

"But we take a higher and a more extended view of this subject, and regard it in its bearing on political economy. And my first remark is, that no nation can be independent which subsists wholly by commerce. And here let it be observed, once for all, that I use the word independent in a sense altogether distinct from sovereignty. I admit that there may be a temporary prosperity; that so long as peace prevails amongst nations connected by commercial and diplomatic relations, — so long as each acts in perfect faith, and maintains in all their entireness and in all their integrity his treaty stipulations, there may not be felt a want of the necessaries or even of the luxuries of life. There may, perhaps, be a large influx of the precious metals. Nothing, however, could be more fallacious, than to regard this activity as an indication of independence or permanent prosperity. For I remark, in the second place, that so uncertain are the operations of trade—so suddenly are its channels and outlets closed by misunderstandings and ruptures between rival nations—so liable is it to paralysing shocks from intriguing cabinets and wily politicians, the operations of one year scarcely afford any ground for conjecture in regard to the operations of the next. Let us illustrate our position by an humble supposition.

"Suppose the surrounding country should suddenly relent, throw wide its doors, and shake its teeming wealth of gold and ivory and wood and gums into our lap; and the native African, patient of labour and of travel, should supply us at the most accommodating rates with all the coarser food for our consumption;—suppose vessels should flock (as, under such circumstances, vessels would most assuredly flock) to our shores, offering us in exchange for the produce thus liberally poured in upon us, the conveniences, elegances, and luxuries of foreign countries. Suppose every man desert his farm, and betake himself to trading as the more easy and the more speedy road to wealth,—there would certainly be great activity and great prosperity. But should we be independent? One more supposition, and the important and interesting problem is solved. Suppose the paths to the interior are suddenly blocked up by feuds among the tribes; all ingress cut off and trade suspended. Where, then, are our supplies? Should we be able to return to our farms, and draw thence articles of exchange with foreign nations? By no means. In the mania for trade our farms have been deserted, and, like the land on which a curse rests, have long laid fallow. Think you, fellow-citizens, that our trade once gone, we should again behold the French, the Bremen, the American, and the English flag floating to the breeze in our harbour. From that hour you might bid a long adieu to every white face but that of a missionary. Fellow-Citizens! our prosperity and independence are to be drawn from the soil. That is the highway to honour, to wealth, to private and national prosperity.

"Liberians! do not disdain the humble occupation! It commends itself to our attention, ennobled and sanctified by the example of our Creator. 'And the Lord God planted a garden eastward in Eden; and there he put the man whom he had formed. And out of the ground made the Lord God to grow every tree that is pleasant to the sight, and good for food.... And the Lord God took the man, and put him into the garden of Eden, to dress it and to keep it.'[3] Never, never, until this degenerate age, has this simple, primitive, patriarchal occupation been despised.

> 'In ancient times, the sacred plough employed
>
> The kings and awful fathers of mankind:
>
> And some, with whom compared your insect tribes
>
> Are but the beings of a summer's day,
>
> Have held the scale of empire, ruled the storm
>
> Of mighty war; then, with unwearied hand,
>
> Disdaining little delicacies, seized
>
> The plough, and greatly independent lived.'

"Thus sings the author of the Seasons, one of Britain's sweetest bards.

"The last remark time will allow me to make under this head, is, that 'Righteousness exalteth a nation; but sin is a reproach to any people.'[4] All attempts to correct the depravity of man, to stay the head-long propensity to vice—to abate the madness of ambition, will be found deplorably inefficient, unless we apply the restrictions and the tremendous sanctions of religion. A profound regard and deference for religion, a constant recognition of our dependence upon God, and of our obligation and accountability to Him; an ever-present, ever-pressing sense of His universal and all-controlling providence, this, and only this, can give energy to the arm of law, cool the raging fever of the passions, and abate the lofty pretensions of mad ambition. In prosperity, let us bring out our thank-offering, and present it with cheerful hearts in orderly, virtuous, and religious conduct. In adversity, let us consider, confess our sins, and abase ourselves before the throne of God. In danger, let us go to Him, whose prerogative it is to deliver; let us go to Him, with the humility and confidence which a deep conviction that the battle is not to the strong nor the race to the swift, is calculated to inspire.

"Fellow-Citizens! we stand now on ground never occupied by a people before. However insignificant we may regard ourselves, the eyes of Europe and America are upon us, as a germ, destined to burst from its enclosure in the earth, unfold its petals to the genial air, rise to the height and swell to the dimensions of the full-grown tree, or (inglorious fate!) to shrivel, to die, and to be buried in oblivion. Rise, fellow-citizens, rise to a clear and full perception of your tremendous responsibilities!! Upon you, rely upon it, depends in a measure you can hardly conceive, the future destiny of your race. You, you are to give the answer, whether the African race is doomed to interminable degradation, — a hideous blot on the fair face of Creation, a libel upon the dignity of human nature, — or whether they are incapable to take an honourable rank amongst the great family of nations! The friends of the colony are trembling; the enemies of the Coloured man are hoping. Say, fellow-citizens, will you palsy the hands of your friends and sicken their hearts, and gladden the souls of your enemies, by a base refusal to enter upon the career of glory which is now opening so propitiously before you? The genius of universal emancipation, bending from her lofty seat, invites you to accept the wreath of national independence. The voice of your friends, swelling upon the breeze, cries to you from afar—Raise your standard! assert your independence!! throw out your banners to the wind!! And will the descendants of the mighty Pharaohs, that awed the world—will the sons of him who drove back the serried legions of Rome and laid siege to the 'eternal city'— will they, the achievements of whose fathers are yet the wonder and admiration of the world—will they refuse the proffered boon, and basely cling to the chains of Slavery and dependence? Never! never!! never!!! Shades of the mighty dead!—spirits of departed great ones! inspire us, animate us to the task—nerve us for the battle! Pour into our bosom a portion of that ardour and patriotism which bore you on to battle, to victory, and to conquest.

"Shall Liberia live? Yes; in the generous emotions now swelling in your bosoms—in the high and noble purpose now fixing itself in your mind, and ripening into the unyieldingness of indomitable principle, we hear the inspiring response—Liberia shall live before God, and before the nations of the Earth.

"The night is passing away—the dusky shades are fleeing, and even now

> 'Second day stands tiptoe
>
> On the misty mountain top.'"

With all their advantages of education and opulence, I challenge the abettors of Negro Slavery, who justify their oppressive conduct towards their fellow-creatures on the ground of their inferiority, to exhibit half the talent and ability evinced in the eloquent addresses of these Coloured legislators. Yet these are the men who are described as a deterioration of our species, who, through vulgar prejudice and popular insult, combined with political and legislative enactments, hove been degraded to a level with the brute.

As further evidence of their capabilities, I present the reader with a few extracts from a Discourse by Henry H. Garnett, (a fugitive Slave), On the Past and Present Condition, and Destiny of the Coloured Race.

"By an almost common consent, the modern world seems determined to pilfer Africa of her glory. It is not enough that her children have been scattered over the globe, clothed in the garments of shame, humiliated and oppressed; but our enemies weary themselves in plundering the tombs of our renowned sires, and in obliterating their worthy deeds, which were inscribed by fame upon the pages of ancient history.

"The three grand divisions of the earth that were known to the ancients, were colonised by the three sons of Noah. Shem was the father of the Asiatics—the Africans descended from Ham—and Japheth was the progenitor of the Europeans. These men, being the children of one common father, they were originally of the same complexion—for we cannot, through the medium of any law of nature or reason, come to the conclusion that one was black, another was copper-coloured, and the other was white. Adam was a red man; and by what law of nature his descendants became dissimilar to him, is a problem which is yet to be clearly solved. The fact, that the universal Father has varied the complexions of his children, does not detract from his mercy, or give us reason to question his wisdom.

"Moses is the patriarch of sacred history. The same eminent station is occupied by Herodotus in profane history. To the chronicles of these two great men we are indebted for all the information we have in relation to the early condition of man. If they are incorrect, to what higher authority shall we appeal; and if they are true, then we acquaint ourselves with the history of our race from that period

'When yonder spheres sublime

Pealed their first notes to sound the march of time.'

"Ham was the first African. Egypt was settled from an immediate descendant of Ham,—who, in sacred history, is called Mizraim, and in uninspired history he is known by the name of Menes. Yet, in the face of this historical evidence, there are those who affirm, that the ancient Egyptians were not of the pure African stock. The gigantic statue of the Sphynx has the peculiar features of the children of Ham; one of the most celebrated queens of Egypt was Nitocris, an Ethiopian woman; yet these intellectual resurrectionists dig through a mountain of such evidence, and declare that these people were not Negroes.

"We learn from Herodotus, that the ancient Egyptians were black, and had woolly hair. These people astonished the world with their arts and sciences, in which they revelled with unbounded prodigality. They became the masters of the East, and the lords of the Hebrews. No arm less powerful than Jehovah's, could pluck the children of Abraham from their hands. The plagues were marshalled against them, and the pillars of cloud and of fire, and at last the resistless sea. 'Then the horse and his rider sank like lead in the mighty waters.'[5] But the kingdom of the Pharaohs was still great. The most exalted mortal eulogium that could be spoken of Moses, was, 'that he was learned in all the wisdom of the Egyptians.'[6] It was from them that he gathered the materials with which he reared that grand superstructure, partaking of law, poetry, and history, which has filled the world with wonder and praise. Mournful reverses of fortune have passed over that illustrious people. The star that rose in such matchless splendour above the eastern horizon has had its setting. But Egypt, Africa's dark-browed queen, still lives. Her pyramid tombs—her sculptured columns, dug from the sands to adorn modern architecture—the remnants of her once impregnable walls—the remains of her hundred-gated city, rising over the wide-spread ruins, as if to guard the fame of the race that gave them existence,—all proclaim what she once was.

"Whatever may be the extent of prejudice against colour, as it is falsely called and is so generally practised in this country, Solomon, the most renowned of kings, possessed none of it. Among the seven hundred wives and the three hundred concubines who filled his houses, the most favoured queen was the beautiful Sable daughter of one of the Pharaohs of Egypt.... When he had secured her, he bowed his great intellect before her, that he might do her that homage which he paid to no other woman. Solomon was a poet, and pure love awakened the sweetest melody in his soul. To her honour and praise he composed that beautiful poem called the Canticles, or Solomon's Song. For her he wove that gorgeous wreath which is unsurpassed in its kind, and with his own royal hand placed it upon her dark brow.

"The interior of Ethiopia has not been explored by modern adventurers. The antiquarian has made his way into almost every dominion where relics of former greatness have promised to reward him for his toil. But this country, as though she had concealed some precious treasure, meets the traveller on the outskirts of her dominions, with pestilence and death. Yet, in the Highlands that have been traversed, many unequivocal traces of former civilization have been discovered. Very lately, British enterprise has made some important researches in that region of country, all of which go to prove, that Homer did not misplace his regard for them, when he associated them with the gods.

"Numerous other instances might be mentioned that would indicate the ancient fame of our ancestors:—a fame, which arose from every virtue and talent that render mortals pre-eminently great,—from the conquests of love and beauty, from the prowess of their arms, and their architecture, poetry, mathematics, generosity, and piety. I will barely allude to the beautiful Cleopatra, who swayed and captivated the heart of Antony;—to Hannibal, the sworn enemy and scourge of Rome—the mighty General who crossed the Alps to meet his foes—the Alps which had never before been crossed by an army, nor ever since, if we except Napoleon, the ambitious Corsican;—to Terence, Euclid, Cyprian, Origen, and Augustine.

"In 1620, the very same year in which the Pilgrims landed on the cold and rocky shores of New England, a Dutch ship, freighted with souls, touched the banks of James river, where the wretched people were employed as Slaves in the cultivation of that hateful weed, tobacco. Wonderful coincidence! The angel of liberty hovered over New England, and the demon of Slavery unfurled his black flag over the fields of the 'sunny south.'

"But, latterly, the Slave-trade has been pronounced to be piracy by almost all of the civilised world. Great Britain has discarded the chattel principle throughout her dominions. In 1824, Mexico proclaimed freedom to her Slaves. The Pope of Rome, and the sovereigns of Turkey and Denmark, and other nations, bow at the shrine of liberty. But France has laid the richest offering upon the altar of freedom, that has been presented to God in these latter days. In achieving her almost bloodless revolution, she maintained an admirable degree of consistency. The same blast of the trumpet of Liberty that rang through the halls of the Tuilleries, and shattered the throne of the Bourbons, also reached the shores of her remotest colonies, and proclaimed the redemption of every Slave that moved on French soil. Thus does France remember the paternal advice of La Fayette, and atone for the murder of Toussaint. Thanks be to God, the lily is cleansed of the blood that stained it. The nations of the earth will gaze with delight upon its democratic purity, wherever it shall be seen, whether in the grape-grown valleys where it first bloomed, or in the Isles of Bourbon, Guadaloupe, Martinique, or in Guiana.[7] The Coloured people of St. Bartholomew's, who were emancipated by a decree of the king of Sweden last year, have lately sent an address to their liberator. Hayti, by the heroism of her Age, Toussaint L'Ouverture, Dessalines, Christophe, and Petion, has driven the demon of Slavery from that island, and has buried his carcase in the sea.

"Briefly and imperfectly have I noticed the former condition of the Coloured race. Let us turn for a moment to survey our present state. The woeful volume of our history, as it now lies open to the world, is written with tears and bound with blood. As I trace it, my eyes ache and my heart is filled with grief. No other people have suffered so much, and none have been more innocent. If I might apostrophise that bleeding country, I would say, O Africa, thou hast bled, freely bled, at every pore! Thy sorrow has been mocked, and thy grief has not been heeded. Thy children are scattered over the whole earth, and the great nations have been enriched by them. The wild beasts of thy forests are treated with more mercy than they. The Libyan lion and the fierce tiger are caged to gratify the curiosity of men, and the keeper's hands are not laid heavily upon them. But thy children are tortured, taunted, and hurried out of life by unprecedented cruelty. Brave men, formed in the divinest mould, are bartered, sold, and mortgaged. Stripped of every sacred right, they are scourged if they affirm that they belong to God. Women, sustaining the dear relation of mothers, are yoked with the horned cattle, to till the soil, and their heart-strings are torn to pieces by cruel separations from their children. Our sisters, ever manifesting the purest kindness, whether in the wilderness of their father-land, or amid the sorrows of the middle passage, or in crowded cities, are unprotected from the lust of tyrants. They have a regard for virtue, and they possess a sense of honour, but there is no respect paid to these jewels of noble character. Driven into unwilling concubinage, their offspring are sold by their Anglo-Saxon fathers. To them, the marriage institution is but a name, for their despoilers break down the hymenial altar and scatter its sacred ashes on the winds.

"Our young men are brutalised in intellect, and their manly energies are chilled by the frosts of Slavery. Sometimes they are called to witness the agonies of the mothers who bore them, writhing under the lash, and as if to fill to overflowing the already full cup of demonism, they are sometimes compelled to apply the lash with their own hands. Hell itself cannot overmatch a deed like this—and dark damnation shudders as it sinks into its bosom and seeks to hide itself from the indignant eye of God."

The writer of the foregoing Discourse was formerly a Slave; his forefathers, stolen from Africa, lived and died in Slavery; he himself was born a Slave, and would have remained in that condition until the present time, had he not been so fortunate as to escape from the galling yoke of fetters and chains. Such an example of elevated humanity as he affords, compels the conviction, that out of the countless millions now doomed to perpetual bondage, many of them, though forcibly degraded to a level with the brute, are qualified to become ornaments, not only to their race but to humanity.

The contents of these pages demonstrate the Negro race to be possessed of intelligent and reflecting minds, capable of occupying a very different station in life to that which has been generally assigned to them, and which they now mostly occupy. Although their sufferings in Slavery have long excited the interest and sympathy of the benevolent, little has been done to advance their position in society. Almost insurmountable obstacles exist, tending to counteract that improvement and elevation of character, to which, under more favourable circumstances, they are capable of attaining.

It may, perhaps, be fairly questioned, whether any other people could have endured the privations or the sufferings to which they have been subjected, without becoming still *more* degraded in the scale of humanity. Nothing has been left undone, to cripple their intellects, to darken their minds, to debase their moral nature, and to obliterate all traces of their relationship to mankind; yet, how wonderfully they have sustained the mighty load of oppression, under which they have been groaning for centuries!

The supporters and advocates of Slavery, in order to justify their oppressive conduct, allege, either in ignorance or from an affected philosophy, an inherent defect in the mental constitution of the Negro race, sufficient to exclude them from the enjoyment of the blessings of freedom, or the exercise of those rights which are equally bestowed by a beneficent Creator upon all his rational creatures.

Prejudice and misinformation have, for a long series of years, been fostered with unremitting assiduity by those interested in upholding the Slave system, and their corrupt influence has enabled them to gain possession of the public ear, and to abuse public credulity to an extent not generally appreciated. They strenuously maintain that the Negro is only fitted and designed for a servile condition. The contents of these pages prove to the contrary, and will surely stop the mouths of those who, from ignorance or something worse, affirm an absolute difference in specific character between the two races, and hence, justify the consignment of the Black to a fate which only proves the fingering barbarism of the White.

But, should the cases here recorded be considered of too isolated a nature to elucidate a theory of general equality of races, it may be observed, that they are only a very fractional part of what might have been adduced. A mass of facts is still in reserve, teeming with unequivocal evidence, that the Almighty has not left the Negro destitute or deficient of those talents and capabilities which he has bestowed upon all his rational creatures, and which, however modified by circumstances in various cases, leave no section of the human family a right to boast that it inherits by birth a superiority, which might not, in the course of events, be manifested and claimed, with equal justice, by those whom they most despise.

In order more fully to demonstrate the capabilities of the Black races of Africa, the writer has selected a mass of facts illustrative of the subject, which he has recently published, entitled "A Tribute for the Negro," in which their moral, intellectual, and religious capabilities are fully established. This

Volume, including many engravings and portraits of eminent Negroes, embraces upwards of one hundred biographical sketches and anecdotes of this calumniated race, many of them not before published, which afford striking evidence that inferior abilities are not the necessary accompaniment of a Coloured skin, but demonstrating, on the contrary, that the Negro race are endowed with every characteristic constituting an identity with the great family of man, and consequently entitled to those inalienable rights which have been denied them, "life, liberty, and the pursuit of happiness," any infringement on which is a daring usurpation of the prerogative of the Most High!

FOOTNOTES:

[1] America.

[2] "Truth is powerful, and will ultimately prevail."

[3] Gen. ii. 8, 9, 15.

[4] Prov. xiv. 34.

[5] Exod. xv. 1, 10.

[6] Acts vii. 22.

[7] The number of Slaves in the French colonies was almost 300,000.